Anderson

the
Ornithologist

First paperback edition 2022

Book design by Sharon Kizziah-Holmes

SOLANDER
PRESS

Published by Solander Press
Rogers, Arkansas
Solanderpress.com

ISBN: 97–8-1-959548-00-3 (paperback)
ISBN 978-1-959548-02-7 (hardcover)
ISBN 978-1-959548-01-0 (eBook)

Dedication

To all the children with autism I have had the pleasure of teaching, you taught me more than you will ever realize.

Acknowledgements

To my Solander Support Group: Linda Apple, Ruth Weeks, Mary Jo Huff and Sharon Kizziah-Holmes.

Anderson
the
Ornithologist

by
Clarissa Willis

illustrations by
Kashif Quasim

SOLANDER
PRESS

I eat lunch alone. Every day. I prefer it that way.

"Can I eat lunch with you?" the new kid asked.

I continued to eat, ignoring the voice. What was I supposed to say? I forgot what I was supposed to say when someone asked a question.

"Can I eat here?" he said a little louder.

I nodded.

He sat down and started to eat. He is a very noisy eater. Noisy eaters annoy me. But I wasn't sure how to tell him to be quieter.

"Cool," Sam said between bites.

"Of course my food is cool. There is nowhere to warm it at school."

"No, it's cool you have a new plate each day, and plastic silverware, too."

"I use a new one for each different food."

"So, what do you do after school?" Sam asked as we threw away our trash.

"I go home." I just stared at him—what a strange question.

"No, I mean, what do you do for fun?"

"I am a junior ornithologist. I like birdwatching.
This weekend I am going to Roaring River
State Park."

Sam was excited. "Wow, camping? Fun."

"No, I am going hunting."

Sam gasped, "Hunting?"

"Yes, with my binoculars, there have been multiple sightings of Dryocopus pileatus."

"That is the name for a pileated woodpecker. They have bright red feathers on their head, and they live deep in the woods. They are very hard to find."

As we walked to class, Sam said, "Sounds like fun. What's your name?"

"Anderson."

"Anderson, can I go?" Sam asked with excitement. "I'll write my phone number down. You can have your mom call my mom. You know, since we are new. Moms like to talk to each other before they let someone new come over."

"Well," I hesitated. This was odd. No one had ever asked to come to my house—ever. "I guess so."

Later that day, Sam handed me a piece of paper with his name and phone number. I didn't have a folder for phone numbers. I decided because he gave it to me after we did math, and since it has numbers on it, the math folder was the best place to put it.

When mom picked me up, she asked, "How was your day?"

"I am not sure."

"Did someone make fun of you again?"

"Not exactly, but something did happen."

"Do I need to talk to your teacher?"

"No, but you do have to call Sam's mother."

"Who is Sam?"

"New kid. He ate lunch with me. Gave me his phone number. He's going birdwatching with us on Saturday."

"He is? Do you want him to go?"

"I think so... Mom? Are you crying?"

"No, just got some dust in my eye."

On Saturday morning Sam's mother dropped him off at our house right on time. I like it when people are on time.

He had his own binoculars, which was great! Mom had told me that I might have to share with Sam. I don't like to share my things.

When we got to the park, we walked around for a long time. Then we heard it—the faint tap-tap-tap of a woodpecker. We followed the noise, and there on a tree right in front of us... not one but three pileated woodpeckers.

Mom took pictures.

"I am going to put my pictures in my birdwatching scrapbook, Sam. What about you?"

"I think I am going to start a scrapbook too," Sam replied.

"Guess what, Sam? I want to go to Papua on the island of New Guinea. There are over 600 different species of birds there. It has one of the largest rainforests in the world!"

"That sounds like fun. I want to go, too."

"Okay."

"Anderson, you know lots of cool things about birds. I think I might want to be an 'orin-bird-watcher' too. I have never had a friend like you before."

I smiled and thought to myself, I've never had a friend.

About Asperger's Syndrome

Asperger's syndrome was a diagnosis used to describe someone on the autism spectrum. It was one of the different types of autism recognized by medical professionals. In 2013, we began to look at autism a little differently. Now Asperger's syndrome is part of an umbrella diagnosis, meaning that autism consists of many different characteristics and behaviors. For this reason, it is called a spectrum disorder. The term Asperger's syndrome is still widely used in educational settings to describe children who often exhibit strong verbal language skills and intellectual ability, as well as some of the other characteristics typically included in the broader definition of autism spectrum disorder. A person with Asperger's syndrome may have repetitive behavior patterns and demonstrate a strong need for routines.

In general, a person with Asperger's syndrome will exhibit some or all of the following characteristics:

- Difficulty making friends or sustaining social interactions
- A very intense interest in one thing or subject
- Desire for predictable routines
- Obvious and unique strengths
- Ability to focus and recognize patterns
- Great attention to detail

Challenges for children with Asperger's syndrome might include some or all of the following:

- Sensitivity to sensory information (sights, sounds, taste, texture)
- Anxiety about new or unique situations
- Difficulty with small talk, especially if the subject matter is not of interest to them
- A preference for one thing (color, food, type of game or activity)
- Difficulty with non-literal communication (Example: When Sam says "cool," Anderson doesn't understand what he means.)
- Misunderstanding social cues, which may lead to being bullied

While the characteristics of Asperger's syndrome vary from one person to another, Anderson has several challenges, such as ongoing issues with social interactions and a strong preference for routines. Like Anderson, many people with Asperger's syndrome will have an intense interest in something atypical for their chronological age. He also has issues with processing information he receives through his senses, such as being annoyed when someone is a noisy eater. Just like Anderson, once you give someone with Asperger's syndrome a chance, they might turn out to be a true and loyal friend.

About the Author

Clarissa Willis, Ph.D., is an author, consultant, and professional developmental specialist. She provides workshops, keynote addresses, and customized professional development nationally and internationally. In her spare time, she writes early childhood curricula, teacher resource books, and books for children. Clarissa has an extensive background in early childhood education. She taught kindergarten and special education, as well as in higher education settings. Clarissa has a Ph.D. in Early Childhood Special Education from the University of Southern Mississippi. She also has a master's degree in Speech-Language Pathology from the University of Arkansas.

She is the author of the best-selling book *Teaching Young Children with Autism Spectrum Disorder*. She has dedicated her career to working with children with autism spectrum disorder and their families. According to Clarissa, "Every child is unique, and I believe that nurturing environments encourage growth, confidence, and success. As a special educator, I know that all children learn best in natural settings."

About the Illustrator

Kashif Qasim is a professional artist living in Pakistan. He has over 20 years of experience in children's book illustration, portraits, landscape art, and sculpture. Fluent in several languages, he works internationally with authors and is best known for his free-hand digital style.